ZAYD SALEEM, CHASING THE DREAM

ON POINT

ZAYD SALEEM, CHASING THE DREAM

BOOK 2

HENA KHAN

ILLUSTRATED BY
SALLY WERN COMPORT

SALAAM
R E A D S

NEW YORK | LONDON | TORONTO
SYDNEY | NEW DELHI

⚙ **SALAAM**
READS

An imprint of Simon & Schuster Children's Publishing Division
1230 Avenue of the Americas, New York, New York 10020
This book is a work of fiction. Any references to historical events, real people, or real places are used fictitiously. Other names, characters, places, and events are products of the author's imagination, and any resemblance to actual events or places or persons, living or dead, is entirely coincidental.
Text copyright © 2018 by Hena Khan
Cover photograph copyright © 2018 by Patrik Giardino
Interior illustrations copyright © 2018 by Sally Wern Comport
All rights reserved, including the right of reproduction in whole or in part in any form.
SALAAM READS and its logo are trademarks of Simon & Schuster, Inc.
For information about special discounts for bulk purchases, please contact Simon & Schuster Special Sales at 1-866-506-1949 or business@simonandschuster.com.
The Simon & Schuster Speakers Bureau can bring authors to your live event. For more information or to book an event, contact the Simon & Schuster Speakers Bureau at 1-866-248-3049 or visit our website at www.simonspeakers.com.
Also available in a ⚙ SALAAM READS hardcover edition
Book design by Dan Potash
The text for this book was set in Iowan Old Style.
The illustrations for this book were rendered in Prismacolor pencil on Denril and digital.
Manufactured in the United States of America
0819 OFF
First ⚙ SALAAM READS paperback edition May 2018
10 9 8 7 6 5 4
Library of Congress Cataloging-in-Publication Data
Names: Khan, Hena, author. | Comport, Sally Wern, illustrator.
Title: On point / Hena Khan ; illustrated by Sally Wern Comport.
Description: New York, New York : Salaam Reads, 2018. | Series: Zayd Saleem, chasing the dream ; 2 | Summary: "Zayd is so excited to finally be on the Gold Team in basketball but when the team starts struggling and his best friend quits to play football he must step up for his team"— Provided by publisher.
Identifiers: LCCN 2017051760 | ISBN 9781534412026 (hardback) | ISBN 9781534412019 (paperback) | ISBN 9781534412033 (eBook)
Subjects: | CYAC: Basketball—Fiction. | Pakistani Americans—Fiction. | Family life— Fiction. | Leadership—Fiction. | Middle schools—Fiction. | Schools—Fiction.|
BISAC: JUVENILE FICTION / Sports & Recreation / Basketball. | JUVENILE FICTION / Family / General (see also headings under Social Issues).
Classification: LCC PZ7.K52652 On 2018 | DDC [Fic]—dc23 LC record available at https://lccn.loc.gov/2017051760

For Bilal
—H. K.

Big-time players lean in, and I am grateful to know a few
—S. W. C.

1

Sometimes when you finally get something you really want, it ends up not being what you hoped it would be. Like that remote-control car that's supposed to be able to drive over anything but gets stuck on the carpet and spins its wheels. Or the haircut that is cool looking on that kid on TV but on you looks like a giant mushroom sprouted on top of your head.

So far, though, being on my new basketball team is as amazing as I thought it would be. It's totally worth the weeks of practice I put into getting ready for tryouts. And that includes getting grounded when I skipped violin practice to play basketball instead. I'm finally on the best team in the fourth-grade league with my best friend, Adam. And each time I lace up my sneakers and step onto the gym floor during practice, I feel like a million bucks.

It's halftime during our first game of the season. My parents and older sister, Zara, are in the stands. I heard them cheering loudly for me when Coach Wheeler put me in during the last five minutes of the first half. I missed a wide-open shot but had a good pass and a nice rebound. And now I get to start the second half!

My heart is thumping wildly in my chest. This is exactly the moment I've been waiting for.

We're huddled around Coach and his clipboard, where he scribbles down plays and taps his pen to make his point. We're down by four. Not too bad. Although by the way Coach is speaking, you'd think we were losing by a lot.

"All right, guys." Coach Wheeler taps on the clipboard. "I know we have new players. We're still learning to work together as a team. That's no excuse for rushing your passes and turning the ball over. Remember to keep the ball up when you rebound."

I look around at my new teammates' faces. Adam looks determined. Blake is super sweaty. Ravindu looks like he hasn't slept enough. And Sam? He's mouthing something to his mom in the bleachers instead of paying attention.

"Who's going to take us home?" Coach asks.

"Let's do this," Adam says gruffly. He's the team captain, and he puts his hand out first. I stick mine on top of his, and soon there's a pile of hands.

"One, two, three, MD HOOPS!" we shout in unison. I feel reenergized as I step back onto the court. I'm going to put up some serious points in the second half. I can feel it.

Blake inbounds the ball, and Adam starts to take it up the court. I always admire his handles. He can dribble behind his back, and he has a sweet crossover. He's stuck right now, though, because the other team is pressing him hard. Two guys are all over him.

"Over here," I yell, holding out my hands. Adam glances at me for a second but then flings the ball over to Blake. A kid from the other team strips it from Blake before he has possession. The kid takes it down the court on a fast break and makes an easy layup. Now we're down by six.

We get the ball back, and this time Adam passes it to me. I immediately have two guys smothering me. All I can see is a bunch of arms waving in my face like a giant octopus. They've got me in a trap, and I try to pass the ball back to Adam. But I turn the ball over. The other team runs down the court and puts up two more points. Now we're down eight.

My dad loves this old movie where this guy wakes up each morning and the same thing happens to him over and over again. It sounds super boring to me, but now I know what he means when he says, "This reminds me of *Groundhog Day*." Because the same exact pattern keeps repeating. We get the ball. They press us. We turn the ball over. They score. Repeat.

We're down by twelve with only three minutes left.

"Time out!" Coach yells. He looks as sweaty as we are and has been pacing the sidelines and yelling louder as each minute ticks by.

"Let's see if you guys have better luck," he mutters as he puts in the entire bench for the rest of the game. Adam and I sit next to Blake, Sam, and Ravindu and watch as our teammates try to shake things up. It doesn't work. We end up losing 32–17.

This isn't how I imagined playing on the gold team would feel. They were undefeated last season and got second place in the playoffs. I thought I'd be playing on *that* team. Today feels like I got another mushroom haircut.

2

"Spicy sauce, please," I say to the guy behind the counter making my pizza. We're at Pie Echo, my new favorite place to eat out. You pick the toppings you want on your pizza, and they put it together and cook it in a super-fast oven that makes the crust bubble and cheese melt in less than five minutes.

This restaurant is perfect for my family since we can never agree on what we want for delivery. Here, Mama can get an entire salad on her pizza, Zara can go crazy with pineapple, and Baba and I can load up on meatballs, jalapeños, and four kinds of cheese. The whole family leaves happy.

"No veggies for you, either, Adam?" Mama looks at Adam's pizza and raises an eyebrow. He came with us for a late lunch after our game. That's been one of the best parts of being on the gold team together. Now we get to hang out even more than before, including carpooling to practice and games. Having Adam at lunch helps to make up for today's loss.

"Tomato sauce is made of veggies," Adam replies with a smile. He's assembled a totally plain cheese pizza. Even I have to admit it looks kind of boring when there are twenty-five different toppings to pick from.

"Whatever you're eating is working," Baba agrees. "You're going to be as tall as me pretty soon!"

Adam's always been taller than me, but suddenly he towers over me by at least a foot. I can't wait until I finally hit that "growth spurt" I always hear about. I've managed to put on a few pounds and finally passed the sixty-pound mark. Even still, the line on the wall in my home where we keep track of my height is hardly budging.

The door opens, and my grandparents come shuffling into the restaurant and look around for us.

"Salaams! You made it!" Zara jumps up to give our grandfather, Nana Abu, her seat and pulls up a chair for Naano. Mama said it would be too hard for them to come to both my game and lunch. So they picked lunch. I don't mind. They don't follow basketball or care much about it, and the bleachers are uncomfortable. Although, I suddenly realize that my uncle, Jamal Mamoo, said he was going to try to be at my game, and he didn't show up.

"Wait, don't sit down. Our pizzas are coming out in a minute. Come up to the counter and let's make yours," Mama says.

Nana Abu sits down anyway and smiles at us.

"We make pizza? They don't make pizza?" Naano asks. She looks appalled.

"No, Naano," I explain. "They make it for you, after you tell them what you want."

"I want onion and mushroom." Naano sits down too.

"What about you, Abu?" Mama asks.

"Anything is fine," he says. Clearly, they aren't interested in walking any farther.

"Okay, come help me, Zayd." While my mom and I are choosing the pizza toppings for my grandparents, Jamal Mamoo walks into the restaurant.

"Hey, Skeletor." He gives me a bro hug and uses his favorite nickname for me. "How was the game?"

"Don't ask."

"Good thing I slept through it, then," he says, laughing. "Mmm. Pizza works for breakfast."

"It's three in the afternoon, Jamal," Mama scolds. "You know this schedule of yours isn't going to work when you're married."

"Married!" I scoff. "Good thing that's not happening anytime soon."

Mama and Jamal Mamoo exchange a look.

"Wait. What's going on?" I ask.

12

"Let's sit down," mamoo says. "I have some news."

Back at the table I feel my pizza gurgling in my stomach as Jamal Mamoo explains that he is getting engaged to Nadia, the girl my family literally JUST went to meet together.

"Mamoo, it's only been, what, a month or two? How can you know you want to marry her already?" I look around at my family. They have to agree that this is madness. Naano and Nana Abu aren't fazed the slightest bit. Zara is beaming at mamoo. Baba seems amused.

I turn to Adam, and he shrugs.

"Dude, don't ask me," he says, his mouth full of pizza.

"Mamoo, really," I say. "Don't you think this is kind of . . . fast?"

"I know it sounds rushed," Jamal Mamoo says.

"What's rushed about it?" Naano says. "I talked to your father two times before we got married."

Adam's jaw drops. "Really?" he whispers to me.

"We've been talking a lot, and we're on the same page about what we want out of life. We laugh a lot, and I know she's the one," Jamal Mamoo continues.

"OH MY GOD!" Zara looks ready to explode. "This is so exciting!"

"I know!" Mama grins. "We're going to have a wedding! We'll get outfits made for the whole family. Maybe the guys can wear suits. Zayd, I wonder where I can get you a suit that isn't too expensive."

"I have a suit I wore last year to my brother's bar mitzvah," Adam offers. "It'll probably fit you."

"Oh, that's nice of you, Adam!" Mama gushes. The rest of lunch all the family wants to talk about is the engagement. Luckily, I have Adam with me. He and I come up with crazy drink combinations at the soda machine since no one is paying attention to us. The best are cherry peach Sprite and vanilla root beer.

It's too bad life doesn't work the same way as the soda fountain or the pizza at Pie Echo. You don't always get to pick what you want. Suddenly mine includes a losing start to the season, a way-too-fast wedding, and a hand-me-down suit.

3

Recess is our reward for having to be at school the whole day. At least it is on the days when it isn't too rainy or too cold to go outside to play. Today is one of those days. I see the sun shining through the window and watch the clock slowly tick down during social studies. I can't wait to rush outside and grab a basketball and a court before they're snatched up.

"What are you doing?" I ask Blake when the bell finally rings and we can line up. He hasn't packed up his stuff.

"I'm not ready for the geography test," Blake says. "I did bad on the review sheet. I need to get help."

"Seriously?" Adam asks. "It's only about directions."

"I got half wrong. I don't get it."

"We can help you. It's easy," I offer. I point in front of us. "If that's north, which way is east?"

"That way," Blake points.

"Right. You got it. Let's go play." I start to leave.

"Wait. Give me another." Blake stops me.

"Okay, if that's north, and you're walking

in the opposite direction, which way are you going?" I say.

"North."

"Dude. I said north is the other way." I give him a friendly punch.

"But I'm facing this way." Blake looks confused.

Adam shakes his head. "There's only one north."

"I know," Blake says. "There's only one north. Which is whichever way I'm facing."

"You think north is whatever way you're facing?" I can't believe what I'm hearing. "You're kidding, right?"

"No. Wait. What do you mean?" Blake turns red.

"Wow," Adam adds. "You can't be serious. Are you serious?"

"You guys are confusing me," Blake whines.

"Go get help, Blake," Adam looks at the clock. "And then hurry up and come outside. We'll be on the court waiting for you. Just head *north*, and you'll find it."

Blake makes a face, and Adam and I rush outside to the basketball court. A bunch of guys are already there, shooting around.

"Where's Blake?" Keanu asks.

"He's . . . uh . . . lost right now." Adam smiles at me. "Let's start without him."

"But we need another," Keanu says.

"Let's play two-on-three until Blake gets here. Me and Zayd versus you three."

"Are you sure?" Chris says.

"Yeah." Adam looks at me. "Right?"

"Sure," I agree, although I don't think it's an even matchup. Keanu and Chris are in the developmental league I used to be a part of. They didn't make the gold team with me, but they're still good. And they have Sam, who's on our team *and* better than me.

But as we start to play, Adam and I are amazing. He starts off by making a smooth bounce pass, setting me up for an easy layup.

"Nice pass," I say as Adam gives me a high five.

The next play I manage to steal the  ball from Keanu, get by Chris, and pass it to Adam. He makes a jump shot near the free throw line. It would be a swish if there were any nets on the hoops.

"Oh yeah!" Adam shouts.

It's as if Adam can read my mind and knows when I'm going to make a move to get open. On the court, I imagine we're my favorite duo, John Wall and Bradley Beal on the Wizards. When they're in sync, they're unstoppable.

"Come on, guys," Chris yells at his teammates. "These two can't beat us."

But we totally do. By a lot. Even without Blake. And when he finally comes out and sheepishly says he understands which way is north now, we're already up by eight. I'm sure that if we play this way during our next game, we'll definitely be headed in the right direction.

4

Everyone is talking at the same time, and no one is listening to each other. They especially aren't listening to Jamal Mamoo, even though we're supposed to be talking about *his* wedding.

"We need to find a caterer or hall with halal food," Mama says.

"Nadia and I were thinking of gourmet southern comfort food," Jamal Mamoo suggests. "Like some shrimp and grits and cornbread."

"Southern food, shmuthern food!" Naano snorts. "If you don't serve proper Pakistani dinner no one will enjoy."

"I want to try shmuthern food," I say.

Zara and I look at each other and smile.

"Butthameez!" Naano scolds me with an Urdu word that means "naughty boy" or something like that.

"Yeah, you're a BUTT-thameez," Zara says, and we both laugh "like hyenas" according to Naano.

"Can we talk about this wedding guest list?" Jamal Mamoo pleads. He doesn't join in the joking like usual. "I don't even know half these people. Nadia and I want to keep it small. Only close friends and family."

"It will be small," Naano says. "Don't take tension. No more than two hundred people."

"Two hundred!" Beads of sweat form on Jamal Mamoo's forehead, and he looks totally stressed out now. "We wanted around seventy-five."

"But your father and I have fifty, and that's only our friends."

"Help me. Please." Jamal Mamoo gives Mama a desperate look. "Nadia's family has to invite their people too. And what about my friends?"

"Let's take a break and have some chai." Mama nods at mamoo and pats him on the shoulder as she gets up to go to the kitchen.

"Can we go outside now?" I ask. Mamoo promised me we'd play some one-on-one, and I've been waiting forever.

"Not yet, Skeletor. We still have a lot of details to work out."

"But this is boring." I can't help complaining. Ever since mamoo mentioned getting engaged, it's the only thing anyone is talking about. And no one has even picked a wedding date yet.

"I know." Jamal Mamoo grimaces. "No one's listening to anything I'm saying anyway. But we need to figure this stuff out. We'll play when we're done."

"Zayd! Can you give me a hand?" Mama calls me from the kitchen before I have a chance to go outside by myself.

I walk into the kitchen, and Mama already has a pot of water and tea leaves simmering on the stove. She pours milk into the pot and stands over it until it starts to boil. I've seen her turn around and not catch the chai from bubbling up and overflowing onto the stove a million times. There's got to be a better way where that doesn't happen. But this is how Naano likes her chai best, and the only way our family makes it.

"Can you get out the sugar and some biscuits?" Mama asks.

I arrange a plate of butter biscuits on a worn metal tray and eat a couple in the process.

"How come mamoo can't make the wedding any way he wants?" I ask when I'm done chewing.

"What do you mean?" Mama asks me, without taking her eyes off the tea.

"I mean he's a grown-up. I get to choose who I want to invite to my birthday parties and what kind of pizza and cake I want. Why doesn't he get to pick what he wants for his own wedding?"

Mama laughs.

"I'm serious," I say. "I don't get it."

"Well . . ." Mama grows thoughtful. "I guess this is more of a team party. Naano and Nana Abu are excited that their only son is getting married, and they want to share their joy with their friends."

"Well the marriage team isn't fun. Jamal Mamoo should quit."

"Shh! Don't give him any ideas. I have my own list of people to invite too. Plus we haven't even talked about decorations or outfits yet."

I look over at Jamal Mamoo, arguing about how he doesn't think he can rent a horse to ride to the wedding like they do in Pakistan. I bet he had no idea this marriage stuff would be this difficult. I hope he figures it out soon. And that he hurries up so we can go outside to play before it gets too dark.

5

"We're going to focus on breaking the press today," Coach Wheeler announces at the start of practice. "That game was rough. We have to work harder to make sure it doesn't happen again."

Everyone sneaks glances at Adam as Coach

speaks. Adam stares straight ahead with a challenging look on his face. It's not exactly fair. The way we lost wasn't only his fault. But since he's our starting point guard, and the one holding the ball most of the time when it got stripped or stolen, he ended up looking the worst.

"Split into two groups," Coach directs us. "Half of you press, and the other half run the press break."

I move with Adam to the press-break group. We have to get the ball to Adam for him to make a move and pass it to someone in the middle of the court. And the other half of the team tries to stop us by being extremely aggressive and not letting us move the ball.

"Go!" Coach shouts.

Cody starts and inbounds the ball. Immediately Blake and Sam start to smother Adam.

He dribbles and tries to cut to his right, but Blake steals the ball from him and takes it down for a fast-break layup. I have a flashback to our *Groundhog Day* game over the weekend. That's exactly what happened to us over and over again.

Coach blows his whistle.

"Adam, try dribbling lower. Make it harder for the other team to steal the ball. Maybe you draw a foul instead of giving up the ball."

"Got it." Adam nods his head.

We start again. This time I inbound the ball past Sam, who is in my face. I barely get it to Adam within the five-second limit.

Adam dribbles between his legs and starts to cut to his left. I run up and get open, Adam makes a quick pass to me, and instantly two guys are covering me tight. I have nowhere to go and try to pass the ball back to Adam. Blake intercepts my pass and is gone again.

"Zayd!" Adam points to where Cody was standing. "You should have passed to Cody."

I didn't see Cody or think he was open. Maybe he was.

"Sorry," I say.

"Guys, listen up. You need to spread out and keep moving. If you end up getting double-teamed, make sure you wait for your teammate to cut and get open. Don't throw a rushed pass." Coach Wheeler sounds as frustrated as I feel.

We run the drill a few more times, and each time something goes wrong. And then we switch up the groups, this time with Sam playing point and us pressing. That goes about the same.

Coach blows his whistle again.

"Let's take a break and work on dribbling and making offensive cuts. Remember, keep the ball low to the floor."

Adam mutters under his breath. "I do keep the ball low."

"Hey," I say to him. "He's saying it to the whole team."

"I know." Adam shakes his head. "But no one gets open. I have nobody to pass to when I'm double-teamed. Our team was much better last season."

Ouch. I don't think he means to say that the team was better before I was on it. Or that it's worse BECAUSE

I'm on it. But his words still sting.

I don't say anything else and work on my moves the way Coach instructs us. We have to figure out how to break the press. And get open quicker. And dribble low. And rebound high. My head is spinning with all the instructions. I'm also going to pray that the next team we play isn't as good as we are. I want the gold team to start winning again. And I want Adam to think this team—with me on it—is even better than the old one.

6

Wednesdays are the best day of the week. Not only do we have gym class in the afternoon, but it's also chorus day. I'm not in the chorus, but since most of my math class is, it means the handful of us that are left get free time. Sometimes we do homework. Or, when Mr.

Thomas is in a good mood, he lets us go to math websites on classroom tablets or do other fun stuff.

"Can we play SMATH?" Adam asks Mr. Thomas. He holds up a box of a math board game.

"Did you finish your worksheet?" Mr. Thomas asks from his desk, where he's grading tests.

"Yup."

"Okay. Keep it down, though. Some of the others are still working."

Adam motions to Blake, Keanu, and me to follow him into the cubby area.

"That game is boring," Keanu complains.

"I know. We're not going to play it," Adam says in a low voice. He pulls a deck of cards out of his backpack. "Grab those Connect Four pieces."

We set the board game up as if we are going to play it. But then we huddle behind it in the cubby area and play poker. Adam divides up the Connect Four pieces as poker chips.

"The black pieces are worth ten dollars, and the red are worth twenty," he explains.

Adam taught me how to play poker during indoor recess earlier in the year. I'm still not that good at it. He's amazing and always seems to win. Win or lose, I'm sure poker is way more fun than SMATH.

"I see your twenty, and I raise you another twenty," Keanu says.

"I'm out," I say as I put down my cards. "I've got nothing."

"Call." Adam puts in his red chip.

"BOYS!" We hear a voice behind us and freeze. It's Mr. Thomas.

"I said you could play the math game! What are you doing?"

"Poker's a math game too," Adam says. "Right? We have to count and stuff."

Mr. Thomas turns red.

"I gave you permission to play SMATH," he says. "But you're being sneaky and playing cards instead?"

"Sorry," we mumble.

"I'm going to have to write you up for being off task and dishonest."

I look at Adam in a panic. I've never gotten a pink slip before. But Adam brushes it off.

Mr. Thomas hands me the slip with a disappointed frown as I leave class for lunch.

"Make sure you show this to a parent and get a signature. And next time I expect you to do what you say you will."

"I will," I say, and then I shove the slip into my binder.

"My parents are going to freak out," I say as I catch up to Adam.

"Just sign it yourself," he says. "That's what I'm going to do."

"No way. I promised my parents to be honest. I'm not getting grounded again." I suddenly realize that when I got into trouble for skipping violin practice to play basketball it was also Adam's idea.

"We were playing cards. You weren't cheating on a test or anything."

I stare at my friend. Why is he acting like he's some tough guy?

"Is everything okay with you?" I ask.

"Yeah. Why?"

"Nothing."

I figure he'll snap out of it. But when we

go out to recess, instead of running to claim a basketball court, he turns to me.

"I'm going to play football with Antonio and Charlie," he says.

"Why?" I can't believe what I'm hearing. We play basketball whenever we go outside.

"I played football yesterday when I was waiting to get picked up after Spanish class, and it was fun."

"Okay." I don't know what else to say, even though it's *not* okay. Not one bit. I pause to see if Adam will ask me if I want to play football with him, but he doesn't. It's not like I want to play with them anyway. Antonio is the biggest kid in the fourth grade, and he plays real football with pads and helmets in some league. I heard he gave a kid a concussion from hitting him too hard. Even though these guys play two-hand touch at recess, they still come

in with grass stains and muddy shoes and scrapes. Besides, I'd rather play basketball any chance I can get.

I watch Adam walk toward the ball rack, pick up a football, and jog off to the field. Between the pink slip and the weird attitude he's having, this Wednesday is the worst.

7

I walk into the house and drop my backpack by the door. Mama and Naano are in the kitchen drinking chai.

"What's the matter?" Mama asks when she sees my face. "You feeling okay?"

I shake my head no.

"What's wrong?" Mama comes close to me and puts her hand on my forehead as if she is checking for a fever.

"I got a . . ."

"What?" Mama looks anxious. "You don't feel warm."

"Pink slip. Even though I didn't do anything bad! Promise. We were playing cards and Mr. Thomas got mad." I say it as quickly as I can.

"What? Show it to me."

"You got a PINK SLIP? Whoa. I *never* got one of those when I was in elementary school."

Zara is sitting at the table eating celery smeared with peanut butter, and she jumps up and comes over to us.

I fumble through my backpack and slowly pull out the pink slip. Zara grabs it out of my hand and starts to read it aloud.

"'Zayd failed to follow directions and stay on task. Please discuss the importance of being honest with him.'"

"Give that to me." Mama holds out her hand. Then she looks at me sternly. "Explain."

"When the people who are in chorus leave, sometimes Mr. Thomas lets the rest of us play games. He said we could play this math game, but we played poker instead."

"You gamble at school?" Naano interrupts. "How much money you make?"

"No, Naano. Not for money. For fun. With Connect Four chips."

"Pshhh." Naano looks disappointed.

"Ammi, let me talk to Zayd, please," Mama pleads. "Remember gambling is haram?"

"That's only if you lose,"

Naano retorts, which makes Mama wince.

"Go on, Zayd," Mama says. "So you weren't playing for money?"

"No! Mr. Thomas got mad at us for not playing the math game."

"What math game?" I can tell Mama doesn't quite believe me.

"It's called SMATH. You make equations. Keanu says it's boring."

"So you played poker instead?"

"Yeah. We were still doing math, kind of. When we were betting. You have to count and stuff."

"You count cards and make lots of money," Naano says with a wink. "I show you how to play twenty-one."

"Ammi, please." Mama frowns, but her eyes are smiling. "And then?"

"Then he caught us and said we were

getting pink slips. He acted like his feelings were hurt."

Mama reads the pink slip and lets out a sigh. I hold my breath, waiting for a lecture on honesty and respect, and wonder what my punishment will be. Then, miraculously, she simply pulls a pen out of the drawer and signs the slip.

"Here you go." She hands it back to me. "Next time do what you said you were going to do. Be good. And don't disappoint your teacher."

"That's it?" I ask.

"Yeah? That's *it*?" Zara asks. She waves her celery in the air. "Doesn't he get in trouble? He got a pink slip!"

"Excuse me, Zara. This doesn't concern you," Mama says. "Zayd, did you learn your lesson?"

"Yeah."

"Okay then. Don't do it again. And I don't want to see any more pink slips."

"Okay."

PHEW! I was expecting a bigger a reaction, but I'll take this. I guess Mama doesn't think sneaking a different game during math is as big a deal as sneaking into the gym to play basketball instead of going to violin lessons for two weeks. And I'm not going to remind her about that.

Naano winks at me again.

"Next time you make money at school, I get half," she says.

Mama sighs louder. I give Naano a high five and then rummage through the pantry for something to eat other than celery.

8

"Did you see the first half of the game last night?" I ask Adam as we file out to recess the next day. "That was crazy when John Wall jumped over those people in the stands. I can't believe he didn't crush anyone."

"Or that he didn't get hurt. My dad says

he's too reckless," Adam says.

"No he isn't. He's amazing," I argue. Wall turned the game around when the Wizards were down by ten, and they came back to win. He's the best point guard I've ever seen. The fans in the stands were shouting "MVP" loud enough for us to hear them on TV.

"Catch you after recess," Adam says, veering away from me.

"What are you doing? You're playing basketball today, right?" I ask, following him.

"Nah. I'm going to play football again." Adam nods over to where Antonio and Charlie are standing by the wall, waiting for him with a football. I realize that means they must have already talked about it.

"But we need you to make the teams even," I protest.

"Ask Ravindu. He'll probably play." Adam points.

I look over to where Ravindu is kicking a soccer ball against the brick wall with another boy. He's good at every sport and on our basketball team. I'm cool playing with him, although it's not the same as playing with Adam.

"Come on." I try to convince him. "We were awesome last time we played at recess. Remember?"

"Yeah." Adam glances at Antonio, who is waving him over. "But . . . those guys are waiting for me."

"We're waiting for you too." What's going on with Adam? Something doesn't feel right.

"I don't get to play football that much. It's fun. Antonio says I'd make an awesome receiver."

"Antonio's not the boss of you." I blurt that out when I can't think of anything else to say.

"Neither are you," Adam snaps back. "Why are you freaking out about this?"

My face gets hot, and I clench my fists tight.

"We ALWAYS play basketball." I kind of yell it. I can't even believe I have to say any of this. We've been playing basketball during recess for two years. It's what we always do.

"Yeah. That's why I'm playing football. Chill, Zayd."

Our team's second game of the season was Sunday afternoon. It was pretty much a repeat of the week before. Anything that could go wrong did. We kept turning the ball over, missing our shots, giving up the fast break, and playing horribly. And we lost 29–15. When we huddled up after the game, Adam wouldn't look at anyone. He looked upset enough to cry. Since I felt the same way, I didn't think anything of it.

But now I ask him, "How are we supposed to figure out how to win again if we don't play?"

"That's what practice is for. I need a break." Adam starts to walk away.

"JOHN WALL WOULDN'T DITCH HIS TEAM!" I shout as I stand there and glare at him.

"WHATEVER!" he barks back without even turning around to look at me.

Maybe Adam doesn't think he's being the worst friend *ever*. But that doesn't change the fact that he is.

"Ravindu! Can you play ball with us?" I pant, out of breath from yelling and running over to him.

"Yeah." Ravindu leaves the soccer ball mid-roll and runs to the court with me.

"Where's Adam?" Blake asks.

"Playing football again," I mutter.

Blake shrugs. "Let's go," he says.

We split up to play three-on-three. It's Ravindu, Chris, and me versus Keanu, Blake, and Sam. Maybe it's because I'm angry with Adam, but something seems to take over me. I'm playing more aggressively than I ever have, boxing out, grabbing every rebound, making crazy passes, and taking shots that I would normally never try. I feel incredible.

But then I look over at the football field and watch Adam catch a long pass.

I get home from school, have a quick snack, and change into my training jersey for practice. Then I lace up the Jordans that Jamal Mamoo got me as a prize for hitting sixty pounds and making the gold team. I never wear them to school since I don't want them to get scuffed or dirty during recess or gym class. I grab a water bottle and my jacket and tell my mom I'm ready to go.

When we get into the car, Mama starts to drive in the direction of practice.

"You forgot to turn. We have to pick up Adam," I say.

"Oh, he didn't tell you?" Mama asks. "His mom texted me to say he's not coming to practice today."

"No." I think back to today. After recess we avoided each other for the rest of the afternoon. It was pretty easy to do since we had to work on our country study and broke into small groups. Adam and I are in different groups. Then, after the bell rang, he rushed out to catch his bus. We didn't talk again.

But now not only did he not play with us at recess, he's not coming to practice, either?

Is it because of our argument? Is he still mad at me? Now I wonder if I shouldn't have said anything to him about playing football and let it go instead. I start to worry. Our team needs Adam like the Wizards need John Wall! And I still need my friend.

When I get to practice, Coach Wheeler sits us on the court and gives us another talk.

"Things didn't go our way last game." He starts by stating the obvious. "But we have to learn from our mistakes and try new things. Today we're going to switch up positions and see if that works better for us."

I've been playing small forward and can't imagine Coach will put me in another position. I'm not tall enough to be center or power forward. That's clearly Matthew or Blake. Adam is our point guard, and Sam subs in for him. I guess maybe I could move

to shooting guard? Coach looks at me first.

"Zayd, I want you on point."

"Me?" I can't help but blurt that out. Is he serious? I look around to see if the rest of the team is as surprised as me. No one seems to think it's a big deal.

"Yeah. Blake, you play center. Ravindu, you're small forward. Sam, you're shooting guard. And Matthew's power forward. You with me?"

"Yes, Coach," we reply in unison. I start to sweat buckets. Me on point? I don't have the handles that Adam does. And to be completely honest, I don't think I'm at Sam's level either. I know I can pass and shoot. I'm trying to be more consistent at getting boards. And I hustle on defense. But putting me in charge of moving the ball up the court? That is not going to help our team start winning. Especially if we get pressed! I don't have the moves to get around two people.

"Let's run four-out," Coach says. I pause for a second, wondering if I should say something to him when no one else is listening? Coach Wheeler won't like being questioned. I imagine the look of disgust on his face if I were to tell him I don't think I'm ready. So I don't.

Coach blows the whistle, and we begin a drill where I start with the ball and then pass it to Ravindu on the wing. Then I run toward Sam and set a screen for him. Ravindu makes a move and passes the ball to Sam. We keep passing the ball around until Matthew makes a shot and it goes in.

"Nice job," Coach says with a nod toward me. "Do it again."

We do the drill over and over. The whole time, I'm comparing myself to Adam. I know he dribbles better than me with his left hand. And he's a lot smoother with his moves. I've always looked up to him for the way he commands the court.

But now Adam isn't here, and I'm left trying to fill his shoes. It doesn't feel right. Besides, what'll happen when he comes back to practice? I hope he won't think it was MY idea and that I tried to steal his spot. I start to sweat again as I picture that scene playing out.

"Let's stick with this for the next week, guys," Coach Wheeler says. "We have a bye week. No game this weekend. So we have more time to prepare. Who wants to take us out?"

I hesitate, and Blake puts his hand out first. The rest of us pile our hands in the middle and shout, "One, two, three, MD Hoops!" I might mumble it. If Adam hasn't been able to lead us to victory, how in the world can I be expected to? I hope he comes back. And quick.

10

My dad has a rule: absolutely no whining or complaining allowed when we go on road trips. Today it's Naano who keeps asking how much longer the ride will be. The rest of the time, she's telling him how to drive. Every couple of minutes she bursts out with "Slow down!" "Watch out!" or "You're too close!" If someone else on the road does something she doesn't like, she rattles off a bunch of curse words in Urdu that I'm pretty sure are way worse than BUTT-thameez.

I can tell by the wrinkles on Baba's forehead and the way he's squishing his lips together that she's frustrating him. And I'm pretty sure that he wants to get to New Jersey as quickly as possible.

My entire family, Jamal Mamoo, Naano, and Nana Abu are crammed into our minivan on an epic adventure to buy stuff for Jamal Mamoo's engagement. It was all Naano's big idea. She heard that the best shop for Pakistani sweets is in this magical place called Edison in New Jersey that I've never been to before.

"We will get mithai and give it to our friends to announce the engagement," she said, while Jamal Mamoo complained.

"Can't we give chocolates instead? No one actually *eats* mithai," he said.

I agreed. I've tried all different types of mithai—pretty much every desi celebration serves it. The colorful super-sweet sweets come in different shapes and flavors. Some are syrupy donuts that are pretty decent. Others are crumbly blocks of candied cheese called burfy. I'm not even making that up. And they taste as gross as that sounds. But Naano made up her mind. She's not going to give up tradition. And she doesn't want any old regular mithai. Nothing but the best will do for her friends, even if that means driving from Maryland to New Jersey for it.

Mama and Zara got super excited about the Indian and Pakistani boutiques and jewelry shops in Edison. Nana Abu and Baba had heard of some famous kabob restaurant called Bundoo Khan they wanted to try. I was probably the least excited about the whole trip, but Mama tried to convince me it would be fun.

"Pretend we're going to Pakistan, without getting on a plane. The shops and restaurants are similar to the ones in Lahore," she said. "We'll get roasted corn and the best kulfi ever."

I've never been to Pakistan and don't know what to expect. Roasted corn and creamy kulfi popsicles don't sound bad, though. I was sold.

Now, after three cramped hours in the car, between Naano's backseat driving, Nana Abu's snoring, and the fact that I left my headphones at home, I'm ready to *get there already*. Jamal Mamoo has hardly talked to me, since he's been texting Nadia Auntie the whole ride.

When we finally pull off the highway, a taxicab cuts us off, and Baba swerves the tiniest bit to avoid it. *SMACK!* Naano grabs the seat in front of her and slams on an imaginary brake with her leg. And then somehow she manages to pray and curse in the same sentence. Zara giggles, and Baba shakes his head.

"We're here," he says with a dramatic hand wave.

We've pulled up in front of Bundoo Khan, which doesn't seem special from the outside. Baba parks on the street, and we pile out of the minivan, tired, hungry, and wrinkled. We file in together, and the smell of masala, fried onions, and barbequed meat hits my nostrils. A man nods us over to a table covered in a clear plastic tablecloth with red placemats underneath.

As we settle in, Nana Abu transforms into someone I've never seen before. My quiet, soft-spoken grandfather is a boss at Bundoo Khan. The waiters rush to him when he looks in their direction, bow their heads when he speaks, and keep asking if there is anything else he wants. He seems to have grown a few inches taller as he orders plates of kabob and rice and asks them to make something that isn't even on the menu.

"What's up with Nana Abu?" I whisper to Zara.

"I don't know," she says. "Maybe it's because it's like we're in Pakistan?"

Then the food starts to come out in metal dishes with handles on them sitting in woven baskets. The reddish tandoori chicken is the best I've ever had in my life—even better than my and Jamal Mamoo's favorite chicken place, Crisp & Juicy. The meat is barbequed perfectly and falls off the bone. It doesn't even need any sauce.

Nana Abu orders naan that has garlic baked

into it and channa masala and curried lamb chops. The dishes keep coming, and we stuff ourselves until my jeans start to feel too tight. It's a spread like Thanksgiving dinner, only a lot spicier. Plus instead of football, there is a cricket match playing on the enormous TV on the wall. When we insist we can't eat any more, the waiters clear the table and bring us glass dishes with rice pudding in them for free.

"This is incredible!" Somehow Zara eats her entire bowl and then finishes Mama's, too. The rest of us can only manage a bite and then look at one another with satisfied-but-slightly-pained expressions. It sounds crazy, but this meal was worth the drive. All three hours of it.

"Let's go," Mama says as she pays the bill. "We have work to do. And we have to make room for kulfi in a few hours."

11

Mama wasn't kidding that Edison could be "Little Pakistan." As we walk down the street, the stores have names like Shalimar Sweets, Saree Bazaar, Maharani Fashions, and Raj Jewels. The mannequins in the windows are wearing fancy shalwar kameezes. Posters of

Bollywood movies and Indian variety shows are plastered everywhere. And there are so many people who look like they could be straight out of Naano's favorite Pakistani dramas walking around.

While Naano, Nana Abu, and Baba head to the sweet store to get mithai, I go with Mama, Zara, and Jamal Mamoo to explore a few boutiques to look for outfits for the wedding.

"Oh, congratulations!" coos a middle-aged woman wearing glasses decorated with sparkling stones when Mama tells her that Jamal Mamoo is getting married.

"Big party?" she asks. Jamal Mamoo shakes his head no, and Mama nods her head yes at the same time.

"Let's see what we have for the handsome groom-to-be," the lady gushes. I can't tell for sure since his skin is dark, but I think Jamal Mamoo might be blushing.

"Check out these shoes, Mamoo," I laugh, holding up a pair of fancy silver slippers that curl up in the front. They resemble what a prince might wear, or the genie from *Aladdin*.

"'A whole new world . . .'" I sing a line from the Disney movie in a fake deep voice, expecting mamoo to bust out with his usual loud wacky laugh. Instead, he barely looks in my direction and continues to listen to the lady make suggestions on the latest in Indian fashion.

"'A new fantastic point of view,'" Zara sings, picking up where I left off. She takes the shoes from me and puts them on. And then we search for other stuff.

I find a super-chunky necklace and a fancy twisted turban and put them on, and Zara finds a bejeweled scarf. We take selfies and videos with Zara's phone and then put all sorts of silly filters on them. We're laughing really hard, and I haven't had this much fun with Zara in a long time. But then Mama calls

her to try on an outfit, and I'm left standing alone in my turban. Mama looks over at me, and her eyes grow big.

"Put that back," she mouths to me.

Mamoo comes out of the dressing room wearing a kurta that is a shimmery dark pink with embroidery on it. There's a cream color scarf draped around his shoulders. He looks at the ladies with a doubtful expression, and they start to gush over him.

"That's perfect," the lady says.

"You think?" mamoo says. "I don't know. It's a bit much."

"Don't you think that's too shiny?" I ask. "Are you seriously letting them dress you up? I thought you were going to wear a suit with me."

Mamoo doesn't even answer me. Instead, he asks Zara to take a picture of him in his getup, and he sends it to Nadia Auntie. Then he gets on the phone with her and starts having a long conversation about what color she will be wearing and what will look good together. Mama is talking to the sparkly eyeglasses lady about the wedding decorations and what will look best, like nothing mamoo says counts at all.

"Can we go now?" I ask my mom.

"In a bit," she says. "Do these look fake?" She holds up a pair of earrings that are in the shape of tiny chandeliers.

"I don't know," I say. And then I pull out my secret weapon. "I need the bathroom."

"Really? You have to go *now*?"

"Yup."

"Can you hold it?"

"No. I have to go bad," I say, putting on a desperate look.

Mama asks the lady if there's a bathroom we can use, and she points to the café across the street. Freedom! We tell Zara and mamoo to meet us there and head over to Agha Juice Bar. I quickly take care of business while Mama orders me a kulfi and herself a falooda, which is a milkshake with red syrup and spaghetti-like noodles in it.

As we walk outside, and I enjoy my sweet milky popsicle, we find the rest of the family standing in front of a man with a cart, putting something together that I've never seen before.

"What is that?"

"It's called paan," Baba says. "It's for grown-ups."

I don't understand how it's for anybody. Paan is a big leaf—as in the thing that comes off a tree. The guy fills the inside of it with a bunch of seeds and syrups and dried coconut that Naano chooses and rolls it up into a tiny triangle burrito. Naano pays him and pops the whole thing into her mouth, which turns a dark orange color from the syrup.

Zara and I look at each other in disbelief as Naano smacks her lips with pleasure. Then she and I go back into the café to get her a kulfi. We help load the mithai and the other packages into the car and start the long drive back. Everyone looks full and satisfied, except for Jamal Mamoo, who falls asleep with his forehead still crinkled up with worry.

12

I've only missed the bus a couple of times before. I ran out of the house and saw the yellow end of the bus turning onto the next street. I tried chasing it the first time, but now I know that I can't catch up. Our driver takes off like she's in a high-speed chase or trying to win the Daytona 500.

Today was another time I missed the bus. I didn't even get outside. Instead, I hit the wrong button on my alarm clock and was still dreaming long after the bus left. Then I heard Baba exclaiming, "Zayd! Get up! What are you still doing in bed?" in my dream. And I opened my eyes and saw him in my doorway with his face half covered in shaving cream and a razor in his hand.

I have a note in my pocket in case I have to sign in at the office, but I dash out of Baba's car and sprint to class right before the bell rings. I'm hot and out of breath, but at least I'm not tardy. Adam looks up as I burst into the room. I haven't seen him since he skipped practice because we didn't have a game scheduled this weekend.

"Hey," I say casually as I pass him on the way to my desk.

"Hey," he replies. I figure things are back to normal, until we line up at lunchtime to go to the cafeteria.

"How come you missed practice?" I ask him. "Were you sick or something?"

"I went to practice with Antonio's team."

"You what?"

"They need a few more players, so Antonio said I could come by and practice with them."

"But the season already started!"

"It's still early enough."

"So what, you're going to play football now?" I say it like I can't believe what I'm hearing. Which I can't.

"Thinking about it." Adam looks at me like he expects me to challenge him. But I don't. We're in the cafeteria now. In my rush to get out of the house this morning, I left my lunch sitting on the counter. I don't say anything else to Adam and stand in line to get a grilled cheese.

Adam heads over to our table and takes a seat with Blake and Keanu. I grab my food and go sit in the spot they've left for me.

"So are you quitting our team, then?" I ask now that we're surrounded by our friends. I know they are going to be as confused as I am.

"Quitting? What are you talking about?" Blake looks at Adam with alarm.

"Why would you quit?" Keanu asks. "Aren't you the star of your team?"

Adam doesn't answer and takes a bite of his sandwich.

"Seriously, dude." Blake presses him. "Why would you quit? We need you."

"He wants to play football," I volunteer.

"I don't know yet," Adam finally says. "I can't do both. The football team practices on the same day twice a week."

"You're going to pick basketball, right? You're team captain," Blake insists. I'm glad he's saying the things I'm thinking. That way I don't have to.

"I don't know. I did awesome at the practice I went to. I love football. And my dad played in high school, so he's excited about it."

"But what about us?" Blake asks.

Exactly. Or more specifically, "What about *me*?" I'm the one who Adam encouraged to try out for his team. I'm the one who worked hard to make it, even when that meant getting grounded in the process. I'm the one who Adam carpools with to games and practices and has fun with. And, oh yeah. I'm also supposed to be his *best friend*.

We stare at him and wait for him to speak. I wonder if he's going to say that basketball isn't as much fun as it was last season. Or that our team isn't as good as it was before. Or that we aren't winning. Because that's got to be why he's doing this, right?

"I'm still friends with you guys even if I play football," Adam finally says. And then he picks up his sandwich again and takes a huge bite.

Blake seems cool with that answer. But I can't help but wonder if Adam even means it, or what's really going to happen. I'm not okay with the way Adam's acting or that he's thinking about quitting our team. But I've learned that chasing the bus doesn't work, and

...nasing Adam, either, or begging him
...n the team with me. I spend the rest
...trying to convince myself that if he
...want to play with me, I don't want to
play with him. Even if I still do.

13

"Zayd, get up. You need to eat breakfast and get ready for your game." Baba sticks his head through my doorway. I don't move and pull the covers over my head instead. A few minutes later he's back.

"Zayd! Come on, buddy. Time to get up. It's

almost ten. What's up with you this week?"

I roll over and stare at the light on the ceiling. My stomach starts to churn. Am I hungry, or is it fear?

"What's the matter? You feeling okay?" Baba comes into my room and sits on the edge of the bed. He starts to poke me.

"My stomach hurts," I mumble.

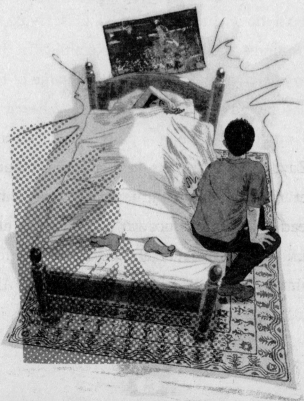

"Nervous about the game?" he asks as he tickles my feet. My family knows that my stomach hurts when I'm anxious about something. At least I don't have to keep a food journal anymore like when Mama tried to figure out if I was allergic to something.

"A little," I confess.

"What do you have to be nervous about? You'll do great." I know Baba is trying to encourage me. How do I explain what I'm nervous about? This is our third game of the season and we are 0–2. Coach Wheeler is planning to put me in at point guard. I've only had a week to practice in this position, and I don't feel good about it. People tend to blame the point guard if you don't win. What if I play worse than Adam, which I probably will?

"Coach has me playing point," I say. "And Adam isn't playing."

"Why not?

"He didn't come to practice this week. He's trying out for football instead."

"That's a shame."

"Yeah. We need him."

Baba looks at me for a second, and then he yanks off my covers.

"Well, the team has other good players. Including you."

"I'm not as good as Adam," I argue.

"You're not going to get any better lying in bed. And if Adam's not there, don't you think your team needs you more than ever?"

"I guess so." I never thought of that.

"Then get up. Coach Wheeler will have a fit if you're late."

When I get dressed and go downstairs, Mama is in the kitchen and has some fruit, yogurt, and granola out.

"Something light to get you moving. Want a smoothie?" she offers.

"No thanks. Who's coming to my game?"

"Just Baba today, sweetie. I have to take Zara to Alison's party. Is that okay?"

"Yeah. Totally." She has no idea how okay it is. I don't want anyone watching me today.

Baba and I pull up at the middle school where our game is being held. I see the other team warming up and feel my stomach turn again. They are so big they could be seventh graders, not fourth graders. I could swear one of them has a mustache. They aren't wearing T-shirts underneath their jerseys, and I can see their muscles flexing. Plus, they clearly know their way around a basketball court.

We warm up for a few minutes, and Coach confirms that he's starting me at point. I know I should be excited. I get to START on the team

I've been dying to be on. But as the seconds tick down to tip-off, my heart starts to beat faster, and I get the sensation that I need to use the bathroom even though I don't. I take a look at the other team's starting lineup. Their center must be at least six feet tall.

The whistle blows, and Matthew gets the ball and passes it to me. I dribble up the court and try not to think too much about what's happening.

All of a sudden the kid who is covering me starts to swipe at the ball as I dribble. I'm forced to stop and look for someone to pass to. Then the kid grabs on to the ball and tries to wrestle it away from me.

The whistle blows. "Jump ball," the ref calls.

This time the other team gets the ball. I run back on defense, and then, as a kid goes up for a shot, I get elbowed in the head.

The ref blows the whistle again.

"You okay?" he asks.

I shake my head no, and Coach Wheeler puts in a sub. On my way to the bench I look at the clock. Only forty-six seconds have passed.

I usually feel restless when I'm on the bench, ready to get back in the game and play again. Today I'm happy to sit out for as long as I can. If there were covers on the bench, I'd pull them over my head and pretend to be asleep when Coach asks me to go back in. I'm not ready to be point guard. And as we deal with another humiliating loss, I wonder if maybe Adam has the right idea after all.

14

I pound the ball on the driveway, working my dribble behind the back, between my legs, and with my left hand. I work on keeping it low to the ground like Coach says we should. It's starting to get a little dark outside, and the lamp is on in the family room. I can see my family through the window, having another wedding planning session with my grand-parents and Jamal Mamoo.

This time I didn't even bother to ask mamoo if he wanted to play one-on-one. I slipped outside after we ate dinner and started to play by myself. So I'm surprised when the garage door opens and mamoo comes out.

"Leaving?" I ask mid-shot. The ball hits the rim, and mamoo grabs the rebound and puts it back.

"Not yet. What are you doing?"

It's weird when adults ask questions that make no sense. Can't he see exactly what I'm doing? I'm guessing he wants me to say something. I don't. Instead, I keep working on my dribbling. Mamoo was never the same as other adults. He always picked playing video games or basketball with me over sitting around with my parents. And we always had a blast when he did weird voices and told the best jokes ever. We'd crack up until our sides ached. But now it's only about Nadia Auntie and this wedding, all the time.

"How was your game today?" mamoo asks when I don't say anything. He holds out his hands, and I toss the ball to him. Or more like chuck it at him. Hard.

"Fine."

"That's not what I heard." Mamoo laughs a little. "I heard it was brutal."

"Who said that?" I ask.

"Your dad."

"Oh."

"He said you were playing point?"

"Yeah."

Mamoo doesn't say anything for a couple of minutes. He stands there and watches me dribble and take a few free throws.

"That's new. Want to play H-O-R-S-E?" he finally says.

"I'm good," I reply, still dribbling.

"You sure?"

"Don't you have wedding planning to do? Or Nadia Auntie to talk to?" I ask.

"Ah. Got it. So that's what's eating you?"

"No."

"Look, Zayd." Mamoo grabs the ball from me and cradles it in his arm. I'm forced to stop and look at him. "I know I've been . . . um, busy recently. But we're still close and always will be. You know that, right?"

"I don't know." Everyone's been acting strange lately. First Adam, and now mamoo.

"Well, we are. And I can't get through this stuff on my own. Did you hear those ladies in there? They are going to drive me nuts. I can't even think straight, and this wedding planning is just starting." Mamoo starts to dribble the ball, hitting it harder against the pavement than he needs to.

"You're the one who wants to get married," I remind him. "Right?"

"Right. I do." Mamoo pauses his dribbling. "You know, you're the one who got me to start talking to Nadia the first day we met, remember? I owe this entire wedding to you."

"No way, Mamoo. This isn't my fault."

Mamoo starts to chuckle a little. I'm not sure what he's finding funny. I hold out my hands, and mamoo throws the ball back to me. And I start working on my crossover. Alone.

Mamoo watches me for a minute and then starts to walk back into the garage. He stops and turns around after a second.

"So are we good, or do I have to tickle you

and make you pee your pants again?" he asks.

"Yeah," I say. I try not to smile as I remember the time he did that.

I wait to see if he tries to play again, but he turns back around and goes inside. I keep playing and thinking about what he said until it's too dark to see the rim.

15

As far as older siblings go, Zara isn't the absolute worst. I've seen some of my friends' older brothers and sisters, and they are pure evil. Sure, Zara can be a know-it-all a lot. And she tattles. But she also plays basketball with me, tries to be helpful, and can be pretty cool when she wants to be. Her friends are another story. I *hate* it when her friends come over, because when they're around, Zara gets meaner to me. She puts on a show for them or, as Naano says, becomes a "show-off."

Today she has not one, not two, but SIX of her friends coming over for an afternoon "spa day." That's what she decided she wanted to do for her thirteenth birthday party. She passed on bowling. Or a bounce place. Or laser tag. Or anything that sounded exciting. Instead, she wants her friends to come over and paint their nails and watch cheesy movies. When I ask Baba about it, he clutches his heart as if he's in pain.

"I'm going to have a teenage daughter on my hands. God help me," he says with a groan.

"Why do they have to come here? Why don't they go to the mall or literally anywhere else?"

"Well this saves a lot of money. I don't mind," Baba says. "It's only a few hours."

Mama, on the other hand, is loving everything about spa day.

"What is *that*?" I ask when I see her mixing up some kind of concoction in the kitchen.

"Cucumber-mint water," she says proudly. "It's very spa-like." I don't see what's special about a jug of water with slices of cucumber and mint leaves floating in it.

"Is it like lemonade?" I wrinkle up my nose.

"Try it." Mama pours a little into a cup and hands it to me.

"Bleh." I spit it into the sink. It takes like the watery part of a cucumber. "This is gross!"

"Well luckily, it's not for you. You and Adam can drink water. Or apple juice."

"Adam?"

"Yeah, his mom texted. She has a work

97

emergency and needs to drop him off here for a couple hours."

"Really?"

"Yes, but listen, Zayd." Mama turns around and gives me a stern look. "No bothering the girls, okay? This is an important day for Zara, and I don't want you to ruin it in any way."

"What? Me?" I act insulted.

"Just let them do their thing, okay?"

"Fine with me. They can paint their nails blue and drink cucumbers all they want." I'm relieved to hear that Adam is coming over. We haven't hung out in ages.

The doorbell rings, and both Zara and I run to the door. It's Alison, holding a glittery gift bag.

"Happy birthday, Zara!" she squeals, even though Zara's birthday isn't actually until Wednesday.

Fifteen minutes later the doorbell rings again, and it's another friend. And then another comes. And then finally it's Adam. He looks confused when he arrives and sees a bunch of shoes in the doorway.

"What's going on?" he asks. "Who's here?"

"Zara's having a weird birthday party," I explain. "Let's go to my room."

We walk up the stairs, and just then someone comes out of the bathroom. It's Alison, with globs of greenish-gray slime all over her face.

"AHHH! It's a zombie!" Adam yells.

"AHHH," I join in.

And then we run downstairs into the family room screaming. When we get there, there is sappy violin music playing and even more girls with gunk on their faces. Except these are lying on the carpet with slices of cucumbers where their eyes are supposed to be. It's not enough to drink cucumbers? They have to *wear* them too? Disgusting.

"There's JUST SO MANY OF THEM!" Adam starts to yell. We can't keep a straight face anymore and start laughing hysterically.

One of the masked people sits up suddenly. The cucumbers tumble off her face.

"Mom!" It's Zara. "Can you make these dorks leave? This is NOT relaxing!"

"Zayd!" Mama marches into the room. "I thought I asked you not to bother the girls."

"Adam started it," I say.

"Please, boys?" Mama begs.

"Yeah. Get out," Zara whines.

We leave, just because Mama asked nicely and because I agreed not to ruin Zara's party. And because I want to get to the basement to play video games before the girls try to claim the TV.

16

"Wanna play 2K?" I ask Adam. Then I suddenly remember his new love for football. "Or I guess Madden?"

"2K's cool."

We settle into the old sofa, and Adam asks me about yesterday's game.

"It was awful," I said. "Pretty much the same as the first two weeks." I pause. "Coach put me in at point. It was his idea."

"How'd you do?" Adam asks.

"Terrible. I turned the ball over a lot. We were pressed again."

"That stinks."

"You decide on a team?" I ask.

"Warriors." Adam selects Golden State as his team, and I of course pick Washington.

"No, I mean in real life. Are you going to do basketball or football?"

Adam hits pause and fiddles with the controller.

"I want to stick with football," he says. "But I don't want people to think I'm a quitter. Or that it's because our team is bad."

"Isn't it?"

"No. I mean it's no fun to lose. But I want

to see if I can play football. And I don't know when else I'll have a chance like this, to be on a team with people I know."

"What if you don't want to stick with football?"

"Then maybe I can come back and get my position back." Adam laughs. He starts our game again.

"That probably won't be too hard." I sigh as Adam makes a sweet three-point shot with Steph Curry.

"Don't underestimate yourself," Adam says. "You're better than you think. You always have been."

"No I haven't."

"Coach wouldn't have picked you for the team otherwise."

"I don't have your handles."

"See? There you go again."

I press a button, and John Wall makes an amazing pass to Marcin Gortat, who dunks it right over Kevin Durant.

"In your face!" I cheer.

"That's what you're best at," Adam says. "You're a good playmaker."

"Yeah, in 2K."

"In real life too. I bet Coach noticed your passing. And you always know where each player is on the court."

"You think?"

"Yeah."

"Thanks, man." It's a relief to know that Adam isn't leaving basketball because of me or how bad our team is. And that he might come back some time. Best of all, he thinks I have what it takes to be on point. He was right about me making the team in the first place. I hope he's right about this, too.

"Yeah, no problem. I just hope I play well on the football team." Adam actually sounds nervous, which makes me look up at him in surprise.

"You're awesome at everything you do," I say. Suddenly I realize that Adam never wanted me to feel bad because he's going after what he wants. And I don't anymore. He should have the chance to play the sport he wants, even if it isn't what I want.

"Except for 2K," I add as I dunk on him again. "I'm a beast. Prepare to lose."

17

"I need your help, guys," Mama says. "We need to get Naano's house ready for the weekend."

"What for?" Zara asks. "What's happening this weekend?"

"Naano invited Nadia Auntie's family to come over to finalize plans for the engagement party and start talking about wedding dates," Mama explains. "Now she's panicking about fixing the yard and taking out the good china and stuff. She can't do it alone."

"Isn't the yard Nana Abu's thing?" I ask. My grandfather loves plants. I can picture him spending hours outside with his tools and coming into the house with his pants covered in dirt.

"His knees hurt him too much now, and he shouldn't be doing any heavy lifting at his age. Come on, we only have a couple hours before it gets dark."

We pull up in front of my grandparents' house, and I notice for the first time that the front garden is a total mess. There are buckets of dead plants around the front door, tools scattered in the mulch, and at least three garden hoses jumbled up. When did this happen?

Naano answers the door.

"Asalaamualaikum," she says. "Ah, you brought my skinny mouse and my strong girl. You two going to work?"

"Yes, Naano," we both say.

"Zara, you help Naano with getting out the dishes. Zayd, you're with me out here," Mama orders. She opens up the trunk of her car and pulls out two pairs of gardening gloves, some yard-waste bags, and a broom and rake.

"I feel bad that I let it go this long," Mama says. "We should have come earlier to help out. Not only because people are coming over."

We spend the next hour digging out the dead plants, hauling away the old containers and tools, and sweeping off the front porch. It looks a lot better when we're done.

"Doesn't that feel good?" Mama says, wiping her hair out of her face with her arm.

"What?" I ask.

"Working with your hands," she says. "Seeing the fruits of your labor."

"I guess so," I say, although I'd rather work on my dribble, and we don't actually have any fruit.

We head inside, and Nana Abu is watching cricket in his favorite armchair in the family room. The volume is turned up super loud, blasting an announcer in a British accent.

"Terrific over," the voice says, although he pronounces "over" as "oh-vah."

"Not for us. Too many runs in that over," Nana Abu grumbles. Then he spots me, and his face lights up.

"Zayd, come watch with me," he says.

"Salaams, Abu," Mama says. "Zayd's here to work today. We're getting ready for the Qureshis' visit."

"They're coming here?" Nana Abu asks. "When?"

"This weekend," Mama says. "Don't you remember we were talking about it?"

"Did we?" Nana Abu smiles. "How nice. We will make sure we host them well. What should I do? I can get down those boxes from the garage that your mother uses."

Mama hesitates, and then she points at me.

"Actually why don't you keep Zayd out of trouble while I help Ammi and Zara in the kitchen," she suggests.

"But you . . ." I start to say that she just said I was here to work, but Mama shakes her head slightly.

"It's okay," she murmurs out of the side of her mouth. "Keep Nana Abu company."

SCORE! I get out of doing anything else!

Watching cricket with my grandfather is

one of my favorite things to do. When I was younger, I didn't understand this sport at all. And Nana Abu didn't explain the rules very well, so I had to figure out what an "over" and a "wicket" were on my own. I didn't understand why the batsmen hold their bats pointing downward. Or why the pitches bounce. And most of all I didn't understand why a game could easily last an entire day. But now I kind of get it, and Nana Abu and I can spend hours yelling at the TV together.

Today as we watch, I notice for the first time how the team captain is really the leader on the field.

"Is he telling them where to go?" I ask Nana Abu.

"Yes. Captain tells the players where to be when they are bowling."

"And does he get to pick who bowls?"

"Of course!"

I can't help but think about how easy this guy makes it look to be in charge. Why can't I be that way? My game is coming up, and I need to find a way to be the one to make a difference.

18

It's game day, and the entire gold team, minus Adam, is sitting in a section of the bleachers. Coach Wheeler ordered us to get there half an hour before game time, and it worked.

"If you wander in ten minutes before the

game, you don't play in the first half," he warned us at practice.

The game before ours hasn't ended yet. We sit and wait for them to clear the court so we can warm up. Coach Wheeler comes over to give us a pregame chat. It's the usual pep-talk kind of stuff. Then he points at me.

"Zayd, you're starting on point. You good with that?"

"Yes, Coach!" I reply as I feel myself start to sweat.

"Good." Coach assigns the rest of the positions. "We're playing the Laurel Lightning. They're good, but they are beatable."

The other game finally ends, and we warm up. As I shoot around, I tell myself the things Coach and Adam have said to me over the past week: "Be aggressive. Don't rush shots. Don't pass when you can drive."

Jamal Mamoo is at the game with my family. I guess he wants to show me that we're still boys, or prove to Mama that he can get somewhere by noon on a Saturday. Either way, I'm glad he's here, and I can hear his loud clapping and screaming "LET'S GO, GOLD TEAM!" over all the talking and cheering.

The ref blows the whistle. It's go time. We huddle up, and Coach asks, "Who wants to take us home?"

This time I don't hesitate, and I put my arm into the middle. "One, two, three, MD HOOPS!" We walk out onto the court, and tip-off goes our way. Blake passes me the ball, and I dribble up the court. There's no press, and I'm able to run the four-out play that Coach likes. *SWISH!* Sam makes an easy bucket. We're off to a good start!

We run back on defense, and Ravindu gets

a steal and makes a layup off a fast break. Our side of the bleachers goes nuts, as if we are in the NBA finals, not the first minute of our fourth game of the season.

"Nice shot!" I yell to Ravindu.

The next possession the Lightning throw the ball out of bounds, and it comes back to us. This time as I take the ball up, they start to double-team me, but I get the ball away in time. We pass the ball around the perimeter until Matthew drives inside and takes a shot. It bounces off the rim, and I grab it, pump fake, and put it back in.

"WOOO-HOOO!" I hear Jamal Mamoo.

We're up 6–0, and we look good. The entire team seems as determined as I am today to get the job done. The Lightning score on their next possession, and we keep going back and forth. We have some good plays and lose the ball a couple of times. They airball a shot and give it back to us for an easy two points.

Coach puts in subs, and I head to the bench and pick up my water bottle.

"I like the toughness," he says to us. "Good control, Zayd." He nods at me.

I look into the stands, and Zara raises her fist. And the rest of my family is grinning like they won the lottery. It's not even halftime, and we're only up by six. But this is the best we've looked the whole season.

Before I know it, halftime is over, and we're back to the starting lineup for the second half. The Lightning get the ball, and we press them, but they manage to get a shot off and it's good.

"That's all right. Get back," I hear Coach yell. Blake inbounds to me, and I take the ball down, looking for an open pass. Blake sets a

screen and stuffs the defender. I get the ball back and see a wide-open lane to the hoop, but also Sam waiting on the wing. I pause for a second, fighting the urge to pass the ball. Then I drive to the hoop and pull up. *SWISH!*

In that moment whatever I was doing to psych myself out disappears. I finally get what it takes to be a good point guard. Sometimes you're there to move the ball. Sometimes you're there to see the open man and get him the ball or take the defense by surprise by driving when they expect you to pass. Getting to be a leader, and to do it all, is the beauty of being the point guard, and why it's my favorite position to see in action. I don't only love watching John Wall. Now I now can try to play like him too. If I'm even a tenth as good, I'll be incredible.

Everyone is hot today. Blake gets an amazing shot and one. Sam gets what I'm convinced is a three-pointer, even though the ref gave him two. Ravindu has three steals. And I have three assists, six points, and only one turn-over. We manage to pull out our first victory of the season. And even though I miss Adam, it still feels amazing. A tiny part of me wonders if it's even better than it would have been with him. That's because now, I'm finally on point.

19

"We have a very good friend who is a doctor in Richmond. He wants to say a few words. Maybe a dua. Or a short ghazl," Nadia Auntie's father says.

Nadia Auntie and Jamal Mamoo look at each other in alarm.

"Abu, we were thinking of no speeches other than the emcee, the imam, and our parents . . . if you feel compelled to say something," Nadia Auntie says.

"No, no," Uncle Qureshi continues. "Dr. Rana always speaks at weddings. He will mind if we don't ask him."

"So the menu is set?" Nadia's mother asks. "Did you pick the caterer?"

"Not yet," Nadia Auntie answers. "We're still working on it."

Naano mutters something in Urdu, but I hear the words "southern shmuthern," and the elders start to chuckle.

Jamal Mamoo turns red.

We're sitting in Naano's living room, in a house that I've never seen this tidy. The stacks of Nana Abu's books and newspapers are put away. There's no pile of medicines or jumbo-size packages of fiber-drink powder on the counter in the kitchen.

We've finished a delicious dinner that Mama and Naano spent three days cooking. And now the wedding planning is happening over chai, fruit, cheesecake, and a variety of mithai that the Qureshis brought over on a fancy silver tray.

"What about the date? It is not good to delay. Why can't we do April?" Naano says.

Nadia Auntie's mom nods in agreement.

"I have to check the kids' spring break schedule," Mama says.

"April is too soon." Jamal Mamoo finally speaks up. "We were thinking May at the earliest. Or June."

"June is too hot," Naano declares.

"Yes, yes, too hot." Nadia Auntie's mom looks like she wants to high-five Naano they are so in sync about the weather.

Jamal Mamoo starts to sweat as if it's June already. Nadia Auntie excuses herself and goes into the hallway near the bathroom. A couple of minutes later, mamoo gets up and follows her. I wait a minute and then sneak out of the room too.

Nadia Auntie and Jamal Mamoo are hanging in the hallway talking in hushed whispers. Nadia Auntie's eyes are huge and she looks panicked, and my uncle is mopping his forehead with a paper napkin. I feel sorry for him. And even though I know it's rude to interrupt them, I can't help it.

"Can I tell you something, Mamoo?" I ask.

"What is it, Skeletor?" Mamoo turns around halfway.

"Zara got to have a spa party for her birthday where they lay around with cucumbers on their eyes, even though I get in trouble for wasting food."

"Um, I'm sorry, Zayd. Can we talk about this later?"

"What I mean is, it didn't matter that I wanted her to pick laser tag. Or that Baba wanted her to stay twelve forever."

"What are you trying to say, Zayd?" Nadia Auntie moves closer to me.

"I mean this is your wedding, right? Not anyone else's. We get to pick what to do for our birthdays that happen every year. And this wedding is a once-in-a-lifetime thing, right?"

"Inshallah." Jamal Mamoo smiles at Nadia, and she gives him a little punch in the arm.

"So stop letting Mama and Naano and Nadia's mom boss you around and tell you what to eat and what to wear and who gets to talk."

"We have to respect their wishes too," Jamal Mamoo says. "It's a family event."

"I know. Mama said that the wedding planning was a big team thing. What I'm saying is you guys need to run point. Let everyone else play and help out. But you have to call the shots. Or else everything is going to stay a big mess like this."

Jamal Mamoo and Nadia Auntie look at each other, and then they smile.

"We're being schooled by a fourth grader, using basketball terms," Nadia Auntie says. "You're totally right, Zayd. I've been too stressed out by all this and not having any fun."

"Me neither," Jamal Mamoo agrees. "I feel pulled in so many directions, and what we want is getting lost."

"So go back in there and be a boss," I say, giving the two of them a gentle shove back toward the living room. "I'm telling you. Trust me."

I didn't do the best job explaining it to them, but I think they got my point. Because if there's one thing I've realized, it's that everyone should have the chance to go after their dreams. Whether it's making a birthday wish with green slime on your face, putting together a wedding that includes what the bride and groom want, trying out a new sport, or stepping up, finding your groove, and turning a losing team around.

"I got this, Skeletor," Jamal Mamoo says as we walk back into the living room. "When did you get so smart all of a sudden?"

"Very funny." I stick my tongue out.

Mamoo puts his arm around me, and somehow that turns into a headlock. I punch him and wiggle out of his grip, and he lets out his wacky laugh. Nadia Auntie and I look at each other and crack up too. As I laugh, I know something for sure. Just like mamoo is going to finally be captain of his wedding team, I'm going to be the next captain of the gold team. And with us in charge, we'll be winners no matter what.

Turn the page for a sneak peek at
Zayd's next on-court adventures!

BOUNCE BACK

My new basketball hoop is going to be amazing. I waited forever to finally replace the rusted, bent rim I've been playing on for the past four years. This one has a clear shatterproof backboard like the ones in the NBA. Plus, there's an adjustable height lever you can use with one hand. I chipped in for half of it using the money I had saved up from my birthday and Eid. My parents paid for the rest.

But after three hours and thirty-seven minutes the hoop is still in pieces all over the driveway. My dad is drenched in sweat. My uncle, Jamal Mamoo, is cursing under his breath and probably wishing he hadn't come over today. And I think my mother is pretending to understand Chinese, since that's the only language in the instruction booklet. She keeps rotating the pages to look at the drawings from different angles.

"I think it's the other end that's supposed to fit in this thingy," Mama says, pointing at the booklet.

"No. It. Doesn't. Go. That. Way." Baba has a washer pressed between his lips and speaks through it in a low growl.

"It's too hot outside," Naano declares from

the doorway of the garage. My grandmother doesn't believe in humans being in the sun for more than five minutes. "How many hours are you going to do this? Stop now. Come have chai."

I look around in alarm, but no one seems ready to quit yet. My family is the kind that loves to watch do-it-yourself shows together on TV. These are the programs about regular people who tear out their kitchen cabinets or showers and install shiny new ones. We comment on their choices and how all the people seem so . . . ordinary. Until they start cutting tiles or using power tools. Then we decide they must secretly be professionals.

The do-it-yourselfers on TV are nothing like the Saleem family. We don't usually fix or build anything ourselves. My parents don't own a toolbox or a single leather tool belt. There's only a sagging shelf in the corner of the garage that holds a hammer, a box of nails, random hooks, and a screwdriver or two.

But it cost an extra seventy-nine dollars to get the hoop assembled. So here we are, putting on a bad reality show for our neighbors. I can't prove it, but it sure feels like they are walking their dogs a lot more than usual today and smiling at us extra hard.

"You guys are doing it wrong." My older sister Zara saunters outside holding a glass of lemonade and wearing a know-it-all look on her face.

"Zara!" Mama snaps her head up from the drawings. "We don't need your commentary right now."

"Okay. I thought you'd want to know I watched a video with instructions. The guy was NOT doing that."

"Wait." Baba turns around and glares at Mama. "There's a video?"

"There's no video listed on here," Mama says, flipping over the booklet. "Unless the link is written in Chinese?"

"What video?" I ask Zara.

"The one on YouTube. I googled it. There's a guy who goes through all the steps one at a time for this exact model basketball hoop. You should watch it. He makes it look easy."

"YOU THINK?" Baba explodes. The lady from two doors down and her tiny yappy dog both jump up, startled as he shouts. I can't help but grin.

Jamal Mamoo catches my eye, drops the pieces of the base he was fumbling to put together, and lets out his wacky laugh. Soon Mama joins in too. Before we know it, we're all howling with laughter. Even Baba. Nana

Abu, my grandfather, comes shuffling outside because of all of the commotion.

"Hold on a second." Mama puts up a hand, gasping for air. "What's so funny?"

Her question just makes us all laugh harder. I drop to the grass and roll around until my stomach hurts, but in a good way.

Two hours and twenty-three more minutes later, I finally get to try out my Spalding X500 hoop.